Young Learner's

Jungle Tales

The Broken Friendship

Goat or Monster?

Goat or Monster?

Once a father goat and a mother goat lived in a tree trunk with their three young children.

One sunny afternoon, as the family was taking a nap, one baby goat began bleating for he was hungry.

A tiger passing by heard the bleating. His mouth began to water at the thought of eating the goat. He began walking in the direction of the sound.
A monkey sitting on the tree saw the tiger and alerted the goat family.

The goat family quickly went inside the trunk. The mother goat and the children got very scared. Father goat was clever and an idea came to his mind. He shouted angrily, “Haven’t you eaten enough already? You have had two wolves and three foxes in the past week, and now you want to eat a tiger!”

By now, the tiger was right in front of the tree. He heard what had been said. He started trembling. He thought, “Maybe, it was a monster that I heard and not a goat. This must be a trap!”

Inside the hollow trunk, the father goat shouted again, “Alright! I will go and get some tigers for you to eat.”

Upon hearing this, the scared tiger ran towards the deep forest to save his life. On the way, he met a fox and told her about the monsters in the trunk. The fox laughed loudly and said, “You have been fooled! A goat family lives in the tree trunk and not any monster. Come with me and I will show you the goats.” The hungry tiger was very angry for he had been fooled. He followed the fox to the tree.

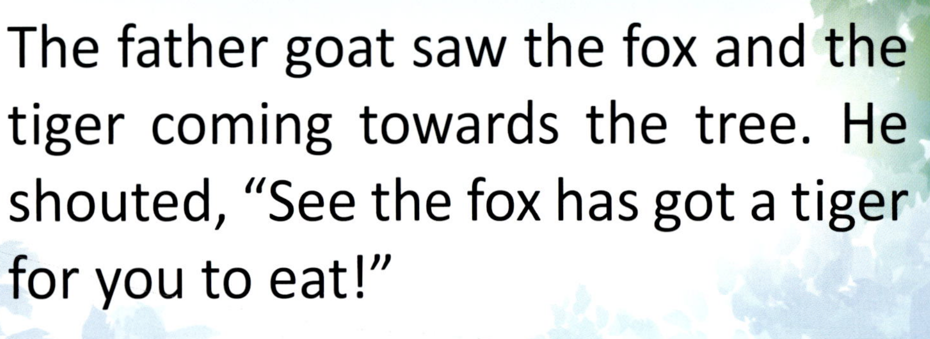

The father goat saw the fox and the tiger coming towards the tree. He shouted, “See the fox has got a tiger for you to eat!”

The tiger thought that the fox had fooled him. He pounced upon the fox and ate her up. He then went away from the forest, never to return. The goats were happy for the dangerous tiger was gone forever.

Moral:
Wisdom is stronger than physical strength.

The Broken Friendship

In a forest lived three bulls. They were the best of friends and were always together. Life was good and the three friends had great time together. A lion had been wanting to eat the bulls for a long time. But he was afraid of attacking them for he knew he could not fight them while they were together. He would often hide and eye them all day while his mouth watered.

One day, he saw the three bulls arguing with each other. All through the day, they stayed together but the lion could see that they were not talking to each other. The lion was very happy! In the evening, the three bulls started shouting at each other.

Finally, they went their separate ways. The lion now had the opportunity he had been waiting for. He followed one of them and attacked him. The bull put up a brave fight but in the end he was defeated. As the bull lay dead on the ground, the lion had a feast for the next many days.

Days passed, and the lion was hungry again. He went looking for the two bulls. He saw one of them grazing in the field.

He thought, “Wow! This one is feeding on lush green grass. I am sure his flesh would be tastier than the one I killed.” He quickly attacked the bull. Unable to fight off the lion, the bull died. The lion was so happy. He had so much meat for himself and his family.

Few days later, the lion hunted the third bull too. That was the end of the three bulls. Till the time they had been together, they were safe. Once they separated, they lost their lives.

Moral:
Unity is strength.